"The Soccer Game

Welcome soccer fans, kids, parents, grammas and gramps.
Who will win this big game and be this year's new champs?

Will the Knights win the game, wearing their white, blue and gold?
They play the game so skillfully and always brave and bold.

**KNIGHTS
2**

**DRAGONS
2**

But the red, white and black play with a strong desire to win.
These Dragons seem to fly and breathe out fire, from within.

The game is tied at two goals each, with five minutes left to go.
Let's catch up with the action, as the excitement begins to grow.

Have fun watching the action, all eyes are on the play.
And practice your reading, to surprise someone today.

Make use of those red letters and blue words, a handy guide.
All the letters have sounds, that make words, along each side.

Practice early reading skills using the special page format.
- see the Literacy Guide chart on page 54 -
4 Building Blocks Of Reading - With Suggested Reading Skills Activities

Sports Action Kids Books - Book 6
ISBN-978-1-7771837-1-4

sportsactionbooks@gmail.com

Copyright © Coach Craig B.Ed. 2020

"Go! Dragons-On-Fire!", some fans cheer up in the stands.

A a
B b
C c
D d
E e
F f
G g
H h
I i
J j
K k
L l
M m
N n
O o
P p
Q q
R r
S s
T t
U u
V v
W w
X x
Y y
Z z

The Dragon players run forward, not looking tired.

"Go! Knights-Are-Heroes!", others shout, clapping their hands.

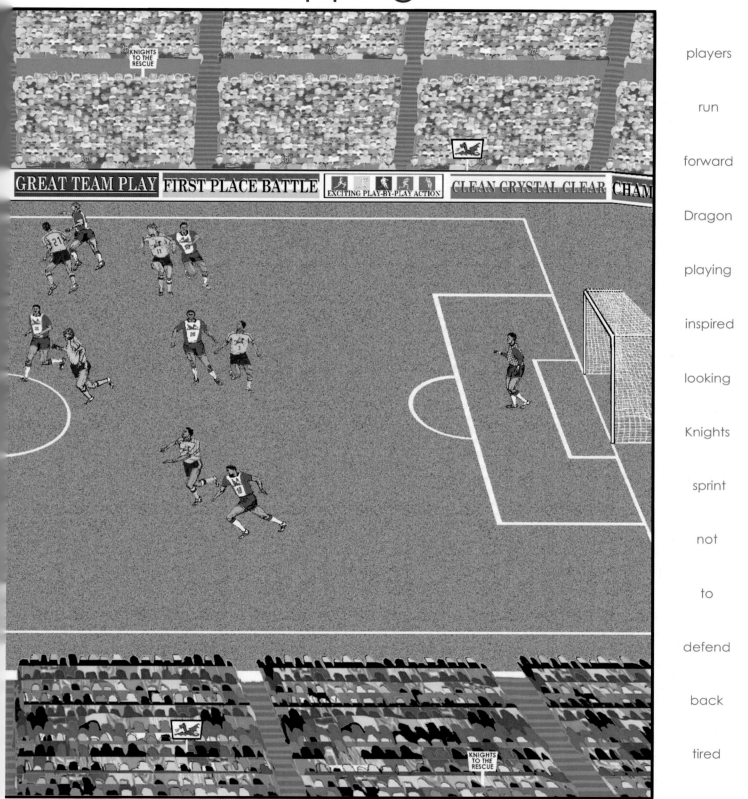

players

run

forward

Dragon

playing

inspired

looking

Knights

sprint

not

to

defend

back

tired

The Knights sprint back to defend, playing so inspired.

A a
B b
C c
D d
E e
F f
G g
H h
I i
J j
K k
L l
M m
N n
O o
P p
Q q
R r
S s
T t
U u
V v
W w
X x
Y y
Z z

The Dragons set up for a throw-in, picking up the pace.

Dragon

throw-in

set

picking

up

for

pace

forward

win

running

moves

space

open

ball

© C.HICKS/2002

A forward running to win
the ball, moves to open space.

A a
B b
C c
D d
E e
F f
G g
H h
I i
J j
K k
L l
M m
N n
O o
P p
Q q
R r
S s
T t
U u
V v
W w
X x
Y y
Z z

Every Knight finds a Dragon,
to follow and guard.

Every Knight finds Dragon follow guard For Dragons have ball charging fast and hard

For the Dragons have the ball, charging fast and hard.

A a
B b
C c
D d
E e
F f
G g
H h
I i
J j
K k
L l
M m
N n
O o
P p
Q q
R r
S s
T t
U u
V v
W w
X x
Y y
Z z

The Dragon crosses the ball with a well placed kick.

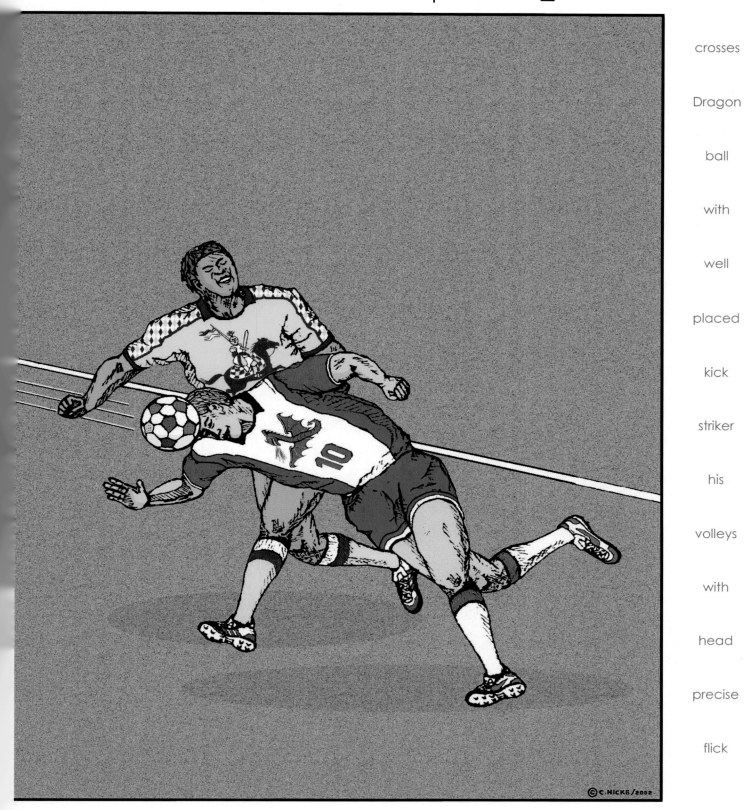

crosses

Dragon

ball

with

well

placed

kick

striker

his

volleys

with

head

precise

flick

His striker volleys it with a precise head flick.

A a
B b
C c
D d
E e
F f
G g
H h
I i
J j
K k
L l
M m
N n
O o
P p
Q q
R r
S s
T t
U u
V v
W w
X x
Y y
Z z

The goalkeeper lunges, as the fans watch in disbelief.

goalkeeper

lunges

the

fans

watch

disbelief

slaps

away

ball

Oooh

cheer

they

relief

big

He slaps the ball away! Oooh!
They cheer in a big relief!

A Knight kicks it away,
no more scoring chances!

Knight kicks it away no more scoring chances midfield players race upfield play advances

The players race upfield, as the play advances.

A a
B b
C c
D d
E e
F f
G g
H h
I i
J j
K k
L l
M m
N n
O o
P p
Q q
R r
S s
T t
U u
V v
W w
X x
Y y
Z z

The Dragons begin to retreat, all moving back.

Dragons

begin

to

retreat

all

moving

back

Knights

control

ball

the

mounting

an

attack

As the Knights control the ball, mounting an attack.

A a
B b
C c
D d
E e
F f
G g
H h
I i
J j
K k
L l
M m
N n
O o
P p
Q q
R r
S s
T t
U u
V v
W w
X x
Y y
Z z

The Knight striker kicks a quick shot, trying to win the match.

Knight

striker

kicks

quick

shot

trying

win

match

Dragon

keeper

set

makes

easy

catch

But the Dragon keeper is set, and makes an easy catch.

"Go! Dragons-On-Fire!",
sing out some fans, all united.

A a
B b
C c
D d
E e
F f
G g
H h
I i
J j
K k
L l
M m
N n
O o
P p
Q q
R r
S s
T t
U u
V v
W w
X x
Y y
Z z

© C. HICKS /2002

Hoof! A good solid kick,
by the Dragon goalkeeper.

"Go! Knights-Are-Heroes!",
chant other fans, all excited.

Hoof

good

solid

by

kick

Dragon

goalkeeper

aims

get

downfield

trying

way

ball

deeper

He aims way downfield,
trying to get the ball deeper.

A a
B b
C c
D d
E e
F f
G g
H h
I i
J j
K k
L l
M m
N n
O o
P p
Q q
R r
S s
T t
U u
V v
W w
X x
Y y
Z z

All the players track the ball,
then three of them jump.

players

track

ball

three

then

them

jump

Dragon

heads

with

passing

it

ball

thump

A Dragon heads the ball, passing it with a thump.

A | a
B | b
C | c
D | d
E | e
F | f
G | g
H | h
I | i
J | j
K | k
L | l
M | m
N | n
O | o
P | p
Q | q
R | r
S | s
T | t
U | u
V | v
W | w
X | x
Y | y
Z | z

A Dragon forward takes the pass, moving to his right.

Dragon forward takes pass moving his right faces two Knight fullbacks their net sight

He faces two Knight fullbacks,
but has their net in sight.

A a
B b
C c
D d
E e
F f
G g
H h
I i
J j
K k
L l
M m
N n
O o
P p
Q q
R r
S s
T t
U u
V v
W w
X x
Y y
Z z

With a challenge from each side,
he looks for an open spot.

challenge

each

side

looks

open

spot

Knight

goalkeeper

Will

Dragon

take

shot

The Knight goalkeeper is set. Will this Dragon take a shot?

A a
B b
C c
D d
E e
F f
G g
H h
I i
J j
K k
L l
M m
N n
O o
P p
Q q
R r
S s
T t
U u
V v
W w
X x
Y y
Z z

Yes! The ball rockets to the net,
a kick indeed well struck.

Yes

ball

rockets

net

kick

well

struck

Wow

makes

keeper

save

little

bit

luck

Wow! The keeper makes the save, with a little bit of luck.

A | a
B | b
C | c
D | d
E | e
F | f
G | g
H | h
I | i
J | j
K | k
L | l
M | m
N | n
O | o
P | p
Q | q
R | r
S | s
T | t
U | u
V | v
W | w
X | x
Y | y
Z | z

A Dragon takes the corner
kick, sending it right in.

Dragon

corner

kick

sending

right

in

ball

flies

high

rising

quick

bending

with

spin

The ball flies up high rising quick, bending with a spin.

A a
B b
C c
D d
E e
F f
G g
H h
I i
J j
K k
L l
M m
N n
O o
P p
Q q
R r
S s
T t
U u
V v
W w
X x
Y y
Z z

The Dragon forwards move in,
ready to get the ball.

But the Knight keeper leaps high, stealing it from them all.

"Go! Dragons-On-Fire!",
some fans cheer up in the stands.

A a
B b
C c
D d
E e
F f
G g
H h
I i
J j
K k
L l
M m
N n
O o
P p
Q q
R r
S s
T t
U u
V v
W w
X x
Y y
Z z

The fans cheer for the keeper,
his saves were astounding.

"Go! Knights-Are-Heroes!", others shout, clapping their hands.

fans cheer for keeper his saves were astounding kicks ball away giving good pounding

He kicks the ball away, giving it a good pounding.

A a
B b
C c
D d
E e
F f
G g
H h
I i
J j
K k
L l
M m
N n
O o
P p
Q q
R r
S s
T t
U u
V v
W w
X x
Y y
Z z

A Knight forward meets the ball,
as it falls from the sky.

Knight

forward

meets

ball

falls

from

sky

controls

great

skill

taking

with

his

thigh

He controls it with great skill, taking it with his thigh.

A a
B b
C c
D d
E e
F f
G g
H h
I i
J j
K k
L l
M m
N n
O o
P p
Q q
R r
S s
T t
U u
V v
W w
X x
Y y
Z z

He spots a Knight ahead, and
leads him nicely with a pass.

spots

Knight

ahead

leads

nicely

pass

Kicking

ball

the

upfield

quickly

rolls

along

grass

Kicking the ball upfield, it quickly rolls along the grass.

A a
B b
C c
D d
E e
F f
G g
H h
I i
J j
K k
L l
M m
N n
O o
P p
Q q
R r
S s
T t
U u
V v
W w
X x
Y y
Z z

Sprinting toward the Dragon net, two Knights break right in.

Sprinting

Dragon

net

Knights

break

in

Trying

hard

score

their

goal

give

team

win

Trying hard to score a goal,
to give their team the win.

Boom! A Knight kicks a hard shot, and the goalkeeper dives.

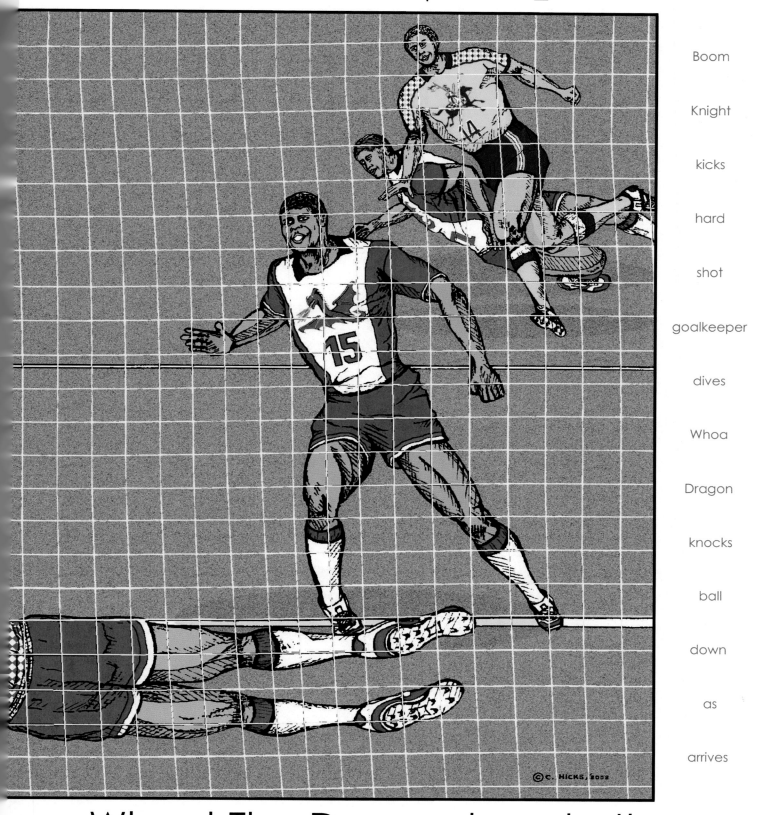

Boom

Knight

kicks

hard

shot

goalkeeper

dives

Whoa

Dragon

knocks

ball

down

as

arrives

© C. HICKS, 2002

Whoa! The Dragon knocks the ball down, just as it arrives.

A a
B b
C c
D d
E e
F f
G g
H h
I i
J j
K k
L l
M m
N n
O o
P p
Q q
R r
S s
T t
U u
V v
W w
X x
Y y
Z z

Wow! What a save! The loose ball now rolls along the ground.

Wow

What

save

loose

ball

rolls

along

ground

players

scramble

quickly

get

big

rebound

© C. HICKS / 2002

The players quickly scramble to get the big rebound.

A a
B b
C c
D d
E e
F f
G g
H h
I i
J j
K k
L l
M m
N n
O o
P p
Q q
R r
S s
T t
U u
V v
W w
X x
Y y
Z z

Whoosh! A Knight kicks the ball
past the keeper. HE SCORES!

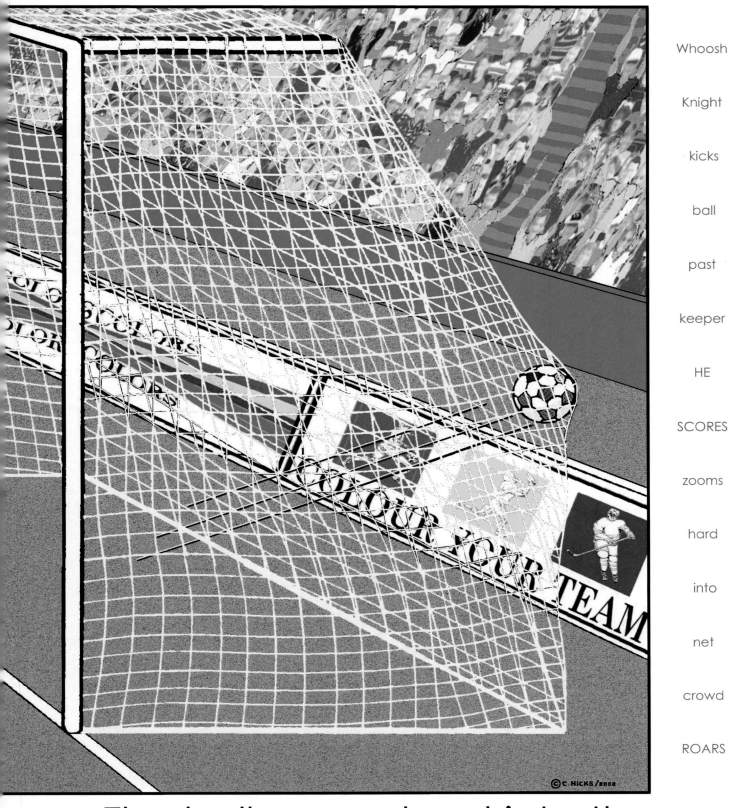

Whoosh

Knight

kicks

ball

past

keeper

HE

SCORES

zooms

hard

into

net

crowd

ROARS

The ball zooms hard into the net, as the crowd ROARS!

Oh! Yeah! Wow! Alright!, shout some fans, they start an uproar!

Wow! The Knights have scored, and now the time runs out.

Oh! No! Geez! Oh-man!, pout other fans, they cheer no more!

Wow

Knights

have

scored

time

runs

out

Knights

win

game

their

fans

scream

shout

The Knights win the game, and their fans scream and shout.

The Dragons and Knights were locked in competition.
Moving upfield and downfield, a grand exhibition.

The players fought hard with no energy to spare.
In the heat of the battle they always played fair.

KNIGHTS

3

DRAGONS

2

The players now walk about and greet one another.
They reach to fist pump, showing respect for each other.

Yes, winning the championship is a sensation.
And, playing with sportsmanship wins admiration.

Grown ups! Let's help the kids learn good reading skills.
Like athletes have coaches for good training drills.

The 4 building blocks of reading are shown in a chart.
Try some of the tips to help make the kids really smart.

Practice early reading skills using the special page format.
- see the Literacy Guide chart on page 54 -
4 Building Blocks Of Reading - With Suggested Reading Skills Activities

Soccer Player Positions

Forwards: - center forward, right forward, left forward, right winger, left winger

>   The players who make up the attacking line or forward line of a team, the center forward, right forward, left forward, right winger and the left winger. These forwards will work together controlling and passing the ball to each other. They will try to get into a position to shoot the ball on the net to try and score a goal. These players are often the fastest players and best dribblers on a team.

Midfielders: - center halfback, right halfback, left halfback

>   The three halfback players who play behind the forwards but in front of the fullbacks, the defenders. They support the forwards when their team is attacking and trying to score and will support the fullbacks and goalkeeper when their team is defending, trying to prevent the other team from scoring.

Defenders: - right fullback, left fullback, goalkeeper

>   The players who play back during the action of a soccer game to defend their zone and goal. They try to stop a goal from being scored and prevent any scoring chances. They check and cover the opposition players who are attacking and trying to score a goal.

Goalkeeper:

>   The player who plays in the goal. He is positioned directly in front of the goal and tries to prevent the ball from getting into the net behind him. This is the only player allowed to use his hands and arms to play the ball to prevent the other team from scoring a goal.

The fans are so excited, on the edge of their seats!

A a
B b
C c
D d
E e
F f
G g
H h
I i
J j
K k
L l
M m
N n
O o
P p
Q q
R r
S s
T t
U u
V v
W w
X x
Y y
Z z

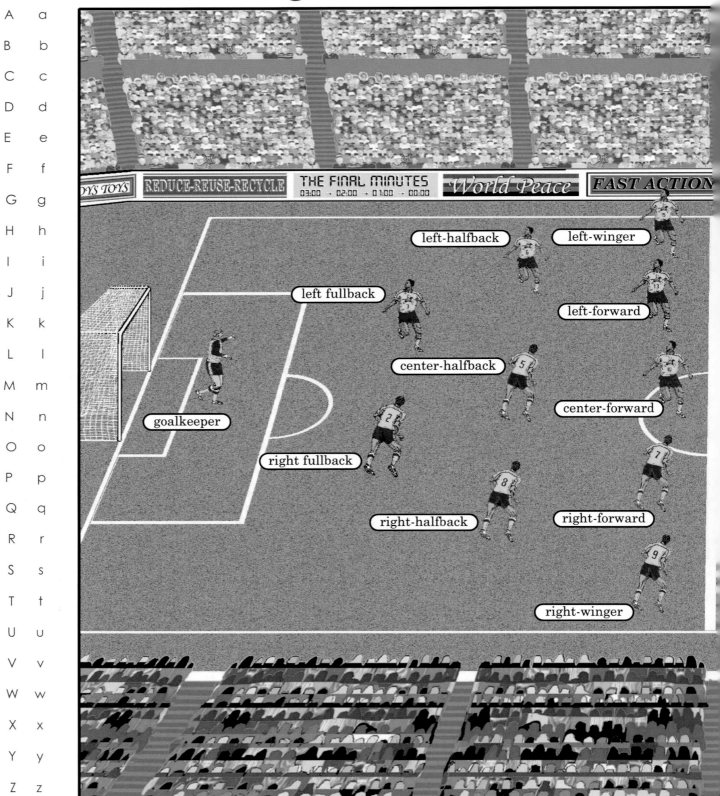

The Knight players move forward to set up their plan.

And they are nervous, no time for cell phone calls or tweets!

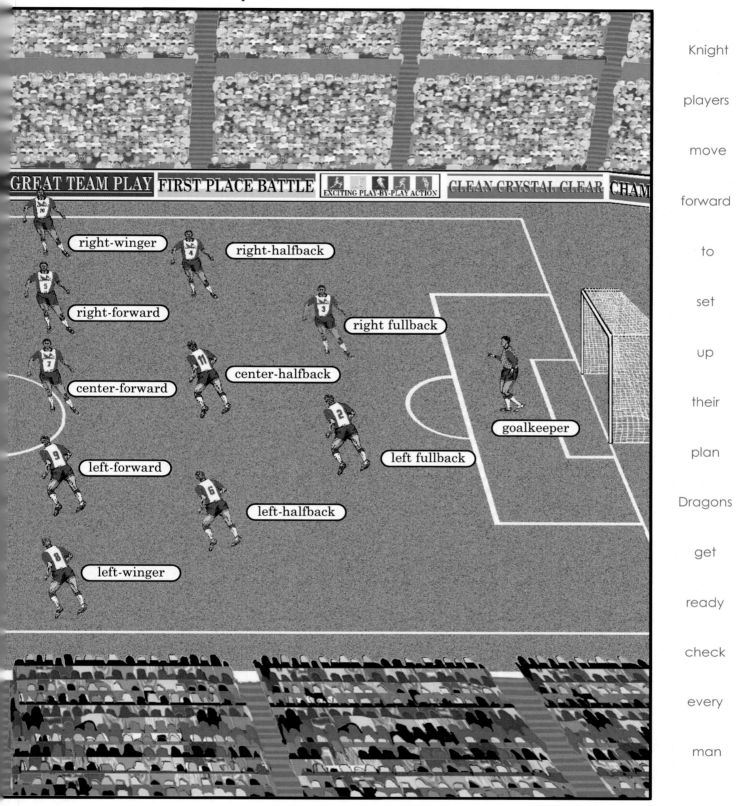

Knight players move forward to set up their plan Dragons get ready check every man

As the Dragons get ready to check every man.

Soccer Glossary

Attack: To advance the ball into your opponents zone in an effort to score a goal.

Attacking team: The team that has possession of the ball.

Bending with a spin: When the soccer ball flies through the air in a curved direction, the spinning of the ball causes it to move to the left or the right.

Break clear: When a player gets to open space to receive a pass or dribble the ball enabling their team to quickly advance the ball down the field.

Challenge: When a player attempts to stop or take the ball away from a player with possession of the ball.

Control the ball: When a player has control of the ball with his feet, dribbling the ball.

Corner kick: When the ball is kicked from the corner in an attempt to score a goal. The attacking team gets a corner kick when the ball crosses the goal line after being touched by the defending team.

Cross or crossing pass: A pass from an attacking player to a teammate in the middle of the field near the goal area, used to give the teammate a good scoring opportunity.

Defenders: The players on the team that try to prevent a goal from being scored on their team. They do not have possession of the ball.

Dribbling: The skill of controlling the ball with the feet while advancing the ball.

Drop kick: When a goalie drops the ball from his hands and kicks it as it falls to his feet.

Field: The rectangular area where a soccer game is played.

Foul: When a player breaks one of the rules for which the referee awards a free kick to the other team.

Goal: A goal is scored when the ball goes between the posts into the net.

Goalkeeper: (goalie) The player who guards the net to prevent the opponents from scoring a goal by stopping the ball any way he can.

Hand ball: A foul when a player touches the ball with his hand or arm. The opposing team is awarded a free kick.

Header: When a player uses his head to contact the ball to control it.

Lead pass: A ball kicked ahead to a teammate running ahead to lead him and advance the ball.

Net: The netting attached to the frame of the goal to trap the ball when a goal is scored.

Offside: An attacking player cannot advance forward without the ball unless an opposing defensive player is between him and the goal he is attacking.

Open spot: A part of the net that is open, not blocked by the goalkeeper, giving an attacking player a chance to score a goal.

Penalty: A punishment given by the referee for a violation of the rules.

Penalty shot: A kick taken by a player against the opposing goalie without any players closer than 10 yards away.

Play advances: When the ball is kicked forward into the opponents end to set up a scoring chance.

Passing: When a player kicks the ball to his teammate to move the ball closer to the opposing goal to score a goal or keep the ball away from an opponent.

Referee: The official in a soccer game. The referee watches all the action closely to make sure all the rules are followed so the game is played fairly. They watch for and call any fouls and make decisions about goals scored.

Retreat: When all the players of a team run back towards their own zone to defend their goal.

Save: When a goalkeeper blocks or stops the soccer ball from going into his team's net.

Scores: When a player kicks the ball into the net of the opposing team for a goal.

Shot: A ball kicked or headed by a player at the opponent's net trying to score a goal.

Sideline: The boundary line that runs the length of the field along each side. A ball is out of play when it crosses the sideline and is out of bounds.

Steal: When a player takes the ball away from an opposing player.

Striker: A team's strongest forward who plays in the center of the field and tries to score goals.

Sweeper: A defender that plays close to his own goal behind the rest of the defenders and in front of the goalkeeper.

Tackling: When a player takes the ball away from another player by kicking or stopping it with his feet.

Throw-in: When a player throws the ball from behind his head with two hands while standing behind a sideline. A throw-in is taken by a player opposite the team that last touched the ball before it went out of bounds.

Volley: When the ball is in the air and is played by a player with his foot or head.

Well struck: When a player kicks the ball with great force making good contact with his foot.

Literacy Guide Chart

Practice early reading skills using the special page format.

-The special page format is designed for children to practice key skills in their reading development.
-The story text is in black, and the alphabet letters in blue on the left, with story words in red on the right.
-This is a handy reference to practice some early reading skills, before, during or after reading the story.

4 Building Blocks Of Reading - With Suggested Reading Skills Activities

-The chart below highlights 4 specific skills that are key building blocks required to produce a new reader.
Use their current ability as a guide to focus on the appropriate skills to practice.

1
Oral Language Development

Speaking aloud and expressing ideas and thoughts builds oral language skills and provides an essential foundation for the development of reading.

Suggested Activities

- look through the story letting the child talk and tell about the pictures using their own words

- encourage, listen and actively respond to the child's own words, thoughts and ideas

-prompt for more oral discussion and detail with questions and rephrasing their words and ideas

-take turns talking about the action and what the players and fans might be feeling, thinking and saying

2
Letter and Sound Recognition

An essential pre-reading skill is recognizing all the letters (upper and lower case) of the alphabet and the sounds that they make.

Suggested Activities

- together point to each blue letter, name and make the sound of each letter in the alphabet

- explain letters have a lower case (small) symbol and upper case (big) symbol

- name a letter, the sound it makes and then have your child point to it (take turns making it a fun game)

- identify a letter and see if it can be found in a red word on the left and in the story (letters make words)

3
Building Word Vocabulary

An important reading skill development is the ability to visually identify words, to recognize the grouping of letters and to remember the word meaning.

Suggested Activities

- point to and say a red word, name each letter and their sounds that group together making each word

- point to and read a red word and then let your child find it in the story sentence (take turns making it a game)

- take turns pointing to and reading aloud each red word from the top to bottom in order

- point to a red word, have your child say the word and explain its meaning (make a sentence with the word)

4
Reading Fluency and Comprehension

Developing the ability to read words accurately and understand their meaning at the same time produces a fluent and competent reader.

Suggested Activities

- read the story together, develop a rhythm and use the rhyme to create and model a natural reading fluency

-ask questions about the action and events to check for memory and understanding

- discuss the thinking, emotions and feelings of the many players and spectators watching the game

- talk about team work, fair-play and sportsmanship, allowing your child to express their feelings and ideas

Find a good balance between working with a child's current abilities and challenging them to learn!
Support literacy development!

Sports Action Kids Books - Book 6
ISBN-978-1-7771837-1-4

sportsactionbooks@gmail.com

Copyright © Coach Craig B.Ed. 2020

Made in the USA
Coppell, TX
10 November 2022

86130417R00033